First published 2017 by Two Hoots.
This edition published 2018 by Two Hoots
an imprint of Pan Macmillan
20 New Wharf Road, London N1 9RR
Associated companies throughout the world
www.panmacmillan.com
ISBN 978-1-4472-7400-1

1 3 5 7 9 8 6 4 2

A CIP catalogue record for this book is available from the British Library. Printed in China
The illustrations in this book were created using pencil and watercolour paint.

www.twohootsbooks.com

For Sonny

Emily Gravett

OLD HAT

TWO HOOTS

Harbet had a hat.

His Nana had
knitted it for
him when he
was little.

It was warm and cosy,
and it kept his ears toasty.

It was an . . .

OLD
HAT!

So Harbet got a new hat.

The latest hat!

It was fashionable, fresh and fun.

It was low in fat,
high in fibre, and
could provide 80%
of his daily vitamins.

It was the latest,
most up-to-datest
hat there was.

Until . . .

It wasn't.

HA HA

So Harbet got a *new* new hat.

This hat really was the latest thing.
It came with a state-of-the-art flashing light
and was highly visible to oncoming traffic.

But when Harbet put on his hat and went outside . . .

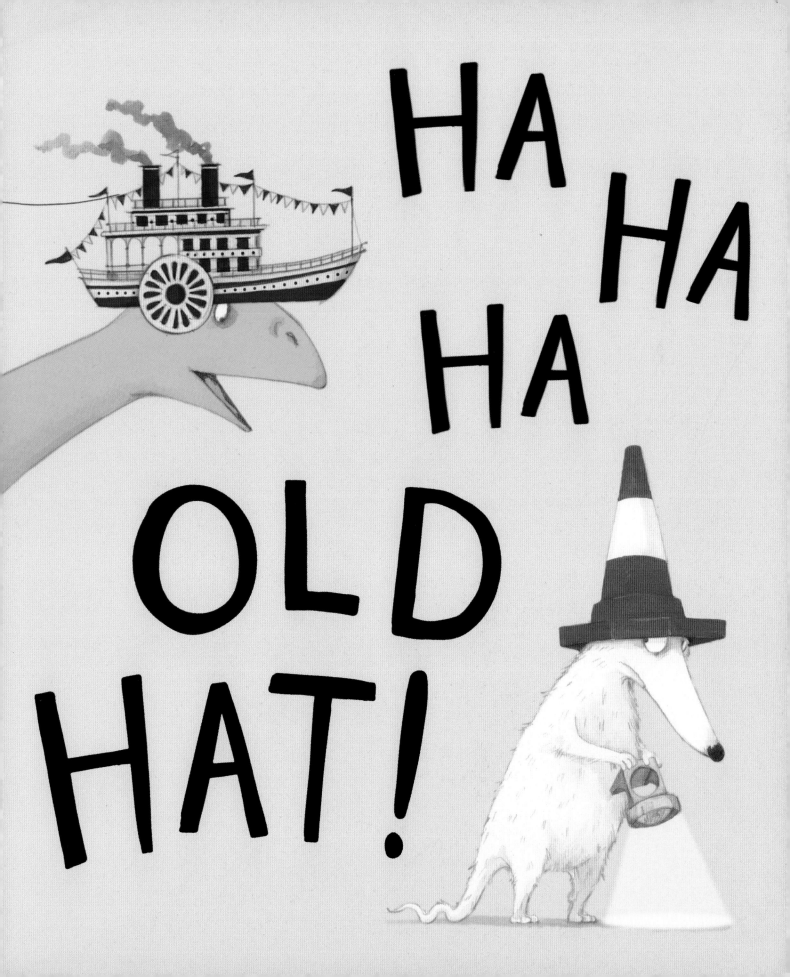

Harbet was determined to have the latest hat.
He bought 'Top Hat' magazine,

and was the first in line at the hat shop
on Hat Unveiling Day.

But whatever Harbet tried . . .

OLD HAT! OLD

HAT! OLD HAT!

Harbet had had enough.

So one day he did something no one had ever done before . . .

Harbet took off his hat.

You may also like one of these stylish ~~books~~ HATS!